I0539071

Devil's Asteroid

Devil's Asteroid
by Manly Wade Wellman

Start Publishing PD LLC
Copyright © 2024 by Start Publishing PD LLC

All rights reserved, including the right to reproduce this book or portions
thereof in any form whatsoever.

Start Publishing PD is a registered trademark of Start Publishing PD LLC
Manufactured in the United States of America

Cover art: Shutterstock/Taisiya Kozorez

Cover design: Jennifer Do

10 9 8 7 6 5 4 3 2 1

ISBN 979-8-8809-0380-1

It was not very large, as asteroids go, but about it clung a silvery mist of atmosphere. Deeper flashes through the mist betokened water, and green patches hinted of rich vegetation. The space-patroller circled the little world knowledgeably, like a wasp buzzing around an apple. In the control room, by the forward ports, the Martian skipper addressed his Terrestrial companion.

"I wissh you joy of yourr new home," he purred. Like many Martians, he was braced upright on his lower tentacles by hoops and buckles around his bladdery body, so that he had roughly a human form, over which lay a strange loose armor of light plates. In the breathing hole of his petal-tufted skull was lodged an artificial voice-box that achieved words. "I rregrret—"

Fitzhugh Parr glowered back. He was tall, even for a man of Earth, and his long-jawed young face darkened with wrath. "Regret nothing," he snapped. "You're jolly glad to drop me on this little hell."

"Hell?" repeated the Martian reproachfully. "But it iss a ssplendid miniaturre worrld—nineteen of yourr miless in diameterr, with arrtificial grravity centerr to hold airr and waterr; ssown, too, with

Terresstrrial plantss. And companionss of yourr own rrace."

accosted

"You! They drive you out?" A thick, unsure voice accosted him.

"There's a catch," rejoined Parr. "Something you Martian swine think is a heap big joke. I can see that, captain."

The tufted head wagged. "Underr trreaty between Marrs and Earrth, judgess of one planet cannot ssentence to death crriminalss frrom the otherr, not even forr murrderr—"

"It wasn't for murder!" exploded Parr. "I struck in self-defense!"

"I cannot arrgue the point. Yourr victim wass a high official perrhapss inssolent, but you Earrth folk forrget how eassy ourr crraniumss crrack underr yourr blowss. Anyway, you do not die—you arre exiled. Prreparre to dissembarrk."

Behind them three Martian space-hands, sprawling like squids near the control-board, made flutelike comments to each other. The tentacle of each twiddled an electro-automatic pistol.

"Rremove tunic and bootss," directed the skipper. "You will not need them. Quickly, ssirr!"

Parr glared at the levelled weapons of the space-hands, then shucked his upper garment and kicked off his boots. He stood up straight and lean-muscled, in a pair of duck shorts. His fists clenched at his sides.

"Now we grround," the skipper continued, and even as he spoke there came the shock of the landfall. The inner panel opened, then the outer hatch. Sunlight beat into the chamber. "Goodbye," said the skipper formally. "You have thirrty ssecondss, Earrth time, to walk clearr of our blasstss beforre we take off. Marrch."

Parr strode out upon dark, rich soil. He sensed behind him the silent quiver of Martian laughter, and felt a new ecstasy of hate for his late guards, their race, and the red planet that spawned them. Not until he heard the rumble and swish of the ship's departure did he take note of the little world that was now his prison home.

At first view it wasn't really bad. At second, it wasn't really strange. The sky, by virtue of an Earth-type atmosphere, shone blue with wispy clouds, and around the small plain on which he stood sprouted clumps and thickets of green tropical trees. Heathery ferns, with white and yellow edges to their leaves, grew under his bare feet. The sun, hovering at zenith, gave a July warmth to the air. The narrow horizon was very near, of course, but the variety of thickets and the broken nature of the land beyond kept it from seeming too different from the skyline of Earth. Parr decided that he might learn to endure, even to enjoy. Meanwhile, what about the other Terrestrials exiled here? And, as Parr wondered, he heard their sudden, excited voices.

Threats and oaths rent the balmy air. Through the turmoil resounded solid blows. Parr broke into a run, shoved through some broad-leafed bushes, and found himself in the midst of the excitement.

A dozen men, with scraggly beards and skimpy rags of clothing, were setting upon an unclassifiable creature that snarled and fought back. It was erect and coarsely hairy—Parr saw that much before the enigma gave up the unequal fight and ran clumsily away into a mass of bright-flowered scrub. Execrations and a volley of sticks and stones speeded its flight.

Then the mob was aware of Parr. Every man—they were all male Terrestrials—turned toward him, with something like respect. One of them, tall and thin, spoke diffidently:

"You just arrived?"

"I was just booted out, ten minutes ago," Parr informed him. "Why?"

"Because you're our new chief," responded the thin man, bowing. "The latest comer always commands here."

Parr must have goggled, for the thin one smiled through tawny stubble. "The latest comer is always highest and wisest," he elaborated. "He is healthiest. Best. The longer you stay on this asteroid, the lower you fall."

Parr thought he was being joked with, and scowled. But his informant smiled the broader. "My name's Sadau—here under sentence for theft of Martian government property."

"I'm Fitzhugh Parr. They said I was a murderer. It's a lie."

One or two chuckled at that, and the one who called himself Sadau said: "We all feel unjustly condemned. Meet the others—Jeffords, Wain, Haldocott...." Each man, as named, bowed to Parr. The final introduction was of a sallow, frowning lump of a fellow called Shanklin.

"I was boss until you came," volunteered this last man. "Now you take over." He waved toward a little cluster of grass huts, half hidden among ferny palms. "This is our capital city. You get the largest house—until somebody new shows up. Then you step down, like me."

He spoke with ill grace. Parr did not reply at once, but studied these folk who were putting themselves under his rule. They would not have been handsome even if shaved and dressed properly. Indeed, two or three had the coarse, low-browed look of profound degenerates. Back into Parr's mind came the words of Sadau: "The longer you stay ... the lower you fall."

"Gentlemen," said Parr at last, "before I accept command or other office, give me information. Just now you were acting violently. You, Sadau, started explaining. Go ahead."

Sadau shrugged a lean freckled shoulder, and with a jerk of his head directed his companions to retire toward the huts. They obeyed, with one or two backward glances. Left alone with Parr, Sadau looked up with a wise, friendly expression.

"I won't waste time trying to be scientific or convincing. I'll give you facts—we older exiles know them only too well. This asteroid seems a sort of Eden to you, I daresay."

"I told the Martians that I knew there was a catch somewhere."

"Your instinct's sound. The catch is this: Living creatures—Terrestrials anyway—degenerate here. They go backward in evolution, become—" Sadau broke off a moment, for his lips had begun to quiver. "They become beasts," he finished.

"What?" growled Parr. "You mean that men turn into apes?"

"Yes. And the apes turn into lower creatures. Those become lower creatures still." Sadau's eyes were earnest and doleful. "The process may run back and down to the worm, for all we can judge. We try not to think too much about it."

"This is a joke of some kind," protested Parr, but Sadau was not smiling.

"Martian joke, perhaps. The treaty keeps them from killing us—and this is their alternative punishment. It makes death trivial by comparison.... You don't believe. It's hard. But you see that some of us, oldest in point of exile, are sliding back into bestiality. And you saw us drive away, as our custom is, a man who had definitely become a beast."

"That thing was a man?" prompted Parr, his spine chilling.

"It had been a man. As you wander here and there, you'll come upon queer sights—sickening ones."

Parr squinted at the huts, around the doors of which lounged the other men. "That looks like a permanent community, Sadau."

"It is, but the population's floating. I came here three months ago—Earth months—and the place was operating under the rules I outlined. Latest comer, necessarily the highest-grade human being, to be chief; those who degenerate beyond a certain point to be driven out; the rest to live peaceably together, helping each other."

Parr only half heard him. "Evolution turned backward—it can't be true. It's against nature."

"Martians war against nature," replied Sadau pithily. "Mars is a dead world, and its people are devils. They'd be the logical explorers to find a place where such things can be, and to make use of it. Don't believe me if you don't want to. Time and life here will convince you."

In the days that followed—the asteroid turned once in approximately twenty-two hours—Parr was driven to belief. Perhaps the slowness of the idea's dawning kept him from some form of insanity.

Every man of the little group that called him chief was on the way to be a man no more. There were stooped backs among them, a forward hang to arms, a sprouting of coarse, lank hair. Foreheads fell away, noses flattened coarsely, eyes grew small and shifty. Sadau informed Parr that such evidences of degeneration meant a residence of a year or so on the exile asteroid.

"We'll be driving one or two of them away pretty soon," he observed.

"What then?" asked Parr. "What happens to the ones that are driven out?"

"Sometimes we notice them, peering through the brush, but mostly they haul out by themselves a little way from here—shaggy brutes, like our earliest fathers. There are lower types still. They stay completely clear of us."

Parr asked the question that had haunted him since his first hour of exile: "Sadau, do you see any change in me?"

Sadau smiled and shook his head. "You won't alter in the least for a month."

That was reasonable. Man, Parr remembered, has been pretty much the same for the past ten thousand years. If a year brought out the beast in the afflicted exiles, then that year must count for a good hundred thousand years turned backward. Five years would be five hundred thousand of reverse evolution—in that time, one would be reduced to something definitely animal. Beyond that, one would drop into the category of tailed monkeys, of rodent crawlers—reptiles next, and then—

"I'll kill myself first," he thought, but even as he made the promise he knew he would not. Cowards took the suicide way out, the final yielding to unjust, cruel mastery by the Martians. Parr stiffened his shoulders, that had grown tanned and vigorous in the healthy air. He spoke grimly to Sadau:

"I don't accept all this yet. It's happened to others, but not to me so far. There's a way of stopping this, and paying off those Martian swine. If it can be done—"

"I'm with you, Chief!" cried Sadau, and they shook hands.

Heartened, he made inquiries. The Martian space-patroller came every month or so, to drop a new exile. It always landed on the plain where Parr had first set foot to the asteroid. That gave him an idea, and he held conference in the early evening, with Sadau, Shanklin, and one or two others of the higher grade.

"We could capture that craft," urged Parr. "There's only a skipper and three Martians—"

"Yes, with pistols and ray throwers," objected Shanklin. "Too big a risk."

"What's the alternative?" demanded Sadau. "You want to stay here and turn monkey, Shanklin? Chief," he added to Parr, "I said once that I was on your side. I'll follow wherever you lead."

"Me, too," threw in Jeffords, a sturdy man of middle age who had been sentenced for killing a Martian in a brawl.

"And me," wound up Haldocott, a blond youth whose skin was burned darker than his hair and downy beard. "We four can pull it off without Shanklin."

But Shanklin agreed, with something like good humor, to stand by the vote of the majority. The others of the community assented readily, for they were used to acting at the will of their wiser companions. And at the next arrival of the Martian patroller—an observer, posted by Parr in a treetop, reported its coming whole hours away—they made a quick disposal of forces around the rocket-scorched plain that did duty for a landing field. Parr consulted for a last moment with Sadau, Shanklin, Jeffords and Haldocott.

"We'll lead rushes from different directions," he said. "As the hatchway comes open, the patroller will stall for the moment—can't take off until it's airtight everywhere. I'll give a yell for signal. Then everybody charge. Jam the tubes by smacking the soft metal collars at the nozzles—we can straighten them back when the ship's ours. Out to your places now."

"The first one at the hatch will probably be shot or rayed," grumbled Shanklin.

"I'll be first there," Parr promised him. "Who wants to live forever, anyway? Posts, everybody. Here she comes in."

Tense, quick-breathing moments thereafter as the craft descended and lodged. Then the hatchway opened. Parr, crouching in a clump of bushes with two followers, raised his voice in a battle yell, and rushed.

A figure had come forward to the open hatch, slender and topped with tawny curls. It paused and shrank back at the sudden apparition of Parr and his men leaping forward. Tentacles swarmed out, trying to push or pull the figure aside so as to close the hatch again. That took more seconds—then Parr had crossed the intervening space. Without even looking at the newcoming exile who had so providentially forestalled the closing of the hatch, he clutched a shoulder and heaved mightily. The Martian whose tentacles had reached from within came floundering out, dragged along—it was the skipper whose ironic acquaintance Parr had made in his own voyage out, all dressed in that loose-plate armor. Parr wrenched a pistol from a tentacle. Yelling again, he fired through the open hatchway. Two space-hands ducked out of sight.

"We've won!" yelled Parr, and for a moment he thought they had. But not all his followers had charged with his own bold immediacy.

Sadau on one side of the ship, Jeffords and Haldocott at the other, had run in close and were walloping manfully at the nozzles of the rocket tubes. The outer metal yielded under the blows, threatening to clog the throats of the blasts. Only at the rear was there no attack—Shanklin, and with him three or four of the lesser men, had hung back. The few moments' delay there was enough to make all the difference.

Thinking and acting wisely, even without a leader, the Martian space-hands met the emergency. They had withdrawn from the open hatchway, but could reach the mechanism that closed it. Parr was too late to jump in after them. Then one of them fired the undamaged rear tubes.

Swish! Whang! The ship took off so abruptly that Parr barely dodged aside in time, dragging along with him the new Terrestrial whose shoulder he clutched, and also the surprised Martian skipper. The rocket blasts, dragging fiery fingers across the plain, struck down Haldocott and Jeffords, and bowled over two of the laggards with Shanklin's belated contingent. Then it was away, moving jumpily with its half-wrecked side tubes, but nevertheless escaping.

Parr swore a great oath, that made the stranger gasp. And then Parr had time to see that this was a woman, and young. She was briefly dressed in blouse and shorts, her tawny hair was tumbled, her blue eyes wide. To her still clung the Martian skipper, and Parr covered him with the captured pistol. Next instant Shanklin, arriving at last, struck out with his club and shattered the flowerlike cranium inside the plated cap. The skipper fell dead on the spot.

"I wanted him for a prisoner!" growled Parr.

"What good would that do?" flung back Shanklin roughly. "The ship's what we wanted. It's gone. You bungled, Parr."

Parr was about to reply with the obvious charge that Shanklin's own hesitancy had done much to cause the failure, when Sadau spoke:

"This young lady—miss, are you an exile? Because," and he spoke in the same fashion that he had once employed to Parr, "then you're our new chief. The latest comer commands."

"Why—why—" stammered the girl.

"Wait a minute," interposed Parr again. "Let's take stock of ourselves. Haldocott and Jeffords killed—and a couple of others—"

Shanklin barked at him. "You don't give orders any more. We've got a new chief, and you're just one of the rabble, like me." He made a heavily gallant bow toward the latest arrival. "May I ask your name, lady?"

"I'm Varina Pemberton," she said. "But what's the meaning of all this?"

Shanklin and Sadau began to explain. The others gathered interestedly around. Parr felt suddenly left out, and stooped to look at the dead Martian. The body wore several useful things—a belt with ammunition and a knife-combination, shoes on the thickened ends of the tentacles, and that strange armor. As Parr moved to retrieve these, his companions called out to halt him.

"The new chief will decide about those things," said Shanklin officiously. "Especially the gun. Can I have it?"

To avoid a crisis, Parr passed the weapon to the girl, who nodded thanks and slid it into her own waist-belt. Shanklin asked for, and received, the knife. Sadau was the only man slender enough to wear the shoes, and gratefully donned them. Parr looked once again at the armor, which he had drawn free of its dead owner.

"What's that for?" asked Shanklin.

Parr made no answer, because he did not know. The armor was too loosely hung together for protection against weapons. It certainly was no space-overall. And it had nothing of the elegance that might make it a Martian uniform of office. Casting back, Parr remembered that the skipper had worn it at the time when he, Parr, was landed—but not during the voyage out. He shook his head over the mystery.

"Let that belong to you," the girl Varina Pemberton was telling him. "It has plates of metal that may be turned to use. Perhaps—" She seemed to be on the verge of saying something important, but checked herself.

"If you'll come with us," Sadau told her respectfully, "we'll show you where we live and where you will rule."

They held council that night among the grass huts—the nine that were left after the unsuccessful attack on the patroller. Varina Pemberton, very pretty in her brief sports costume, sat on the stump that was chief's place; but Shanklin did most of the talking.

"Nobody will argue about our life and prospects being good here," he thundered, "but there's no use in making things worse when they're bad enough." He shook a thick forefinger at Fitzhugh Parr, who wore the armor he had stripped from the dead

Martian. "You were chief, and what you said goes. But you're not chief now—you're just the man who murdered four of us!"

"Mmm—yes," growled one of the lower-fallen listeners, a furry-shouldered, buck-toothed clod named Wain. "That blast almost got me, right behind Haldocott." His eyes, grown small, gleamed nastily at Parr. "We ought to condemn this man—"

"Please," interposed Sadau, who alone remained friendly to Parr, "it's for the chief to condemn." He looked to Varina Pemberton, who shook her head slowly.

"I feel," she ventured with her eyes on Parr, "that this ought to be left up to you as a voting body."

Shanklin sprang to his feet. "Fair enough!" he bawled. "I call Parr guilty. All who think like me, say aye!"

"Aye!"

"Aye!"

"Aye!"

They were all agreeing except Sadau, who looked shrunken and sad and frightened. Shanklin smirked.

"All who think he should be killed as a murderer—"

"Hold on," put in Varina Pemberton. "If I'm chief, I'll draw the line there. Don't kill him."

Shanklin bowed toward her. "I was wrong to suggest that before a woman. Then he's to be kicked out?"

There was a chorus of approving yells, and all save Sadau jumped up to look for sticks and stones. Parr laid his hand on the club he had borne in the skirmish that day.

"Now wait," he said clearly and harshly, and the whole party faced him—Sadau wanly, the girl questioningly, the rest angrily.

"I'm to be kicked out," Parr repeated. "I'll accept that. I'll go. But," and the club lifted itself in his right hand, "I'm not going to be rough-housed. I've seen it happen here, and none of it for me."

"Oh, no?" Shanklin had picked up a club of his own, and grinned fiercely.

"No. Let me go, and I leave without having to be whipped out of camp. Mob me, and I promise to die fighting, right here." He stamped a foot on the ground. "I'll crack a skull or two before I wink out. That's a solemn statement of fact."

"Let him go," said Varina Pemberton again, this time with a ring of authority. "He wears that armor, and he'll put up a fight. We can't spare any more men."

"Thank you," Parr told her bleakly. He gave Shanklin a last long stare of challenge, then turned on his heel and walked away toward the thickets amid deep silence. Behind him the council fire made a dwindling hole in the blackness of night. It seemed to be his last hope, fading away.

He pushed in among thick, leafy stems. A voice hailed him:

"Hah!"

And a figure, blacker than the gloom, tramped close to him across a little grassy clearing.

"You! They drive you out?" a thick, unsure voice accosted him.

Parr hefted his club, wondering if this would be an enemy. "Yes. They drove me out. I'm exiled from among exiles."

"Uh." The other seemed perplexed over these words, as though they stated a situation too complicated. Parr's eyes, growing used to the darkness, saw that this was a grotesque, shaggy form, one of the degenerate outcasts from the village. "Uh," repeated his interrogator. "You come to us. Make one more in camp. Come."

Among tall trees, thickly grown, lay a throng of sleepers. Parr's companion led him there, and made an awkward gesture.

"You lie down. You sleep. Tomorrow—boss talk. Uh!"

So saying, the beast-man curled up at the root of a tree. Parr sat down with his back against another trunk, the club across his knees, but he did not sleep.

This, plainly enough, was the outcast horde. It clung together, the gregariousness of humanity not yet winnowed out by degeneration. It had a ruler, too—"Tomorrow boss talk." Talk of what? In what fashion?

Thus Parr meditated during the long, moonless night. He also took time to examine once more his captured armor. Its metal plates, clamped upon a garment of leatheroid, covered his body and limbs, even the backs of his hands, as well as his neck and scalp. Yet, as he had decided before, it was no great protection against violence. As clothing it was superfluous on this tropical planetoid. What then?

He could not see, but he could feel. His fingers quested all over one plate, probing and tapping. The plate was hollow—in reality, two saucer-shaped plates with their concave faces together. They gave off a muffled clink of hollowness when he tapped them. When he shook the armor, there was something extra in the sound, and that impelled him to hold a plate close to his ear. He heard a soft, rhythmic whirr of machinery.

"There's a vibration in this stuff," he summed up in his mind. "What for? To protect against what?"

Then, suddenly, he had it.

The greatest menace of the whole tiny world was the force that reversed evolution—the vibration must be designed to neutralize that force!

"I'm immune!" cried Fitzhugh Parr aloud; and, in the early dawn that now crept into the grove, his sleeping companions began to wake and rise and gape at him.

He gaped back, with the shocked fascination that any intelligent person would feel at viewing such reconstructions of his ancestors. At almost the first glance he saw that the newest evolutionary thought was correct—these were simian, but not apes. Ape and man, as he had often heard, sprang from the same common fore-father, low-browed, muzzle-faced, hairy. Such were these, in varying degrees of intensity. None wore clothes. Grinning mouths exhibited fanglike teeth, bare chests broadened powerfully, clumsy hands with short, ineffectual thumbs made foolish gestures. But the feet, for instance, were not like hands, they were flat pedestals with forward-projecting toes. The legs, though short, were powerful. Man's father, decided Parr, must have had something of the bear about his appearance ... and the most bearlike of the twenty or thirty beast-men heaved himself erect and came slouching across toward Parr.

This thing had once been a giant of a man, and remained a giant of an animal. None of the others present were nearly as large, nor were any of the men who had driven Parr forth. Six feet six towered this hair-thicketed ogre, with a chest like a drayhorse, and arms as thick as stovepipes. One hand—the thumb had trouble opposing the great cucumber fingers—flourished a club almost as long as Parr's whole body.

"I—boss," thundered this monster impressively. "Throw down stick."

Parr had risen, his own club poised for defense. The giant's free hand pointed to the weapon. "Throw down," it repeated, with a growl as bearlike as the body.

"Not me," said Parr, and ducked away from the tree-trunk against which he might be pinned. "What's the idea? I didn't do anything to you—"

"I—boss," said his threatener again. "Nobody fight me."

"True, true," chorused the others sycophantically. "Ling, he boss—throw down club, you new man."

Parr saw what they meant. With the other community, the newest and therefore most advanced individual ruled. In this more primitive society, the strongest held sway until a stronger displaced him. The giant called Ling was by no means the most human-seeming creature there, but he was plainly the ruler and plainly meant so to continue. Parr was no coward, but he was no fool. As the six-foot bludgeon whirled upward between him and the sky, he cast down his own stick in token of surrender.

"No argument, Ling," he said sensibly.

There was laughter at that, and silly applause. Ling swung around and stripped bare his great pointed fangs in a snarl. Silence fell abruptly, and he faced Parr again. "You," he said. "You got on—" And he stepped close, tapping the plates on Parr's chest.

"It's armor," said Parr.

"Huh! Ah—ar—" The word was too much for the creature, whose brain and mouth alike had forgotten most language. "Well," said Ling, "I want. I wear."

He fumbled at the fastenings.

Parr jumped clear of him. He had accepted authority a moment ago, but this armor was his insurance against becoming a beast. "It's mine," he objected.

Solemnly Ling shook his great browless head, as big as a coal-scuttle and fringed with bristly beard. "Mine," he said roughly. "I boss. You—"

He caught Parr by the arm and dragged him close. So quick and powerful was the clutch that it almost dislocated Parr's shoulder. By sheer instinct, Parr struck with his free fist.

Square and solid on that coarse-bearded chin landed Parr's knuckles, with their covering of armor plate. And Ling, confident to the point of innocence because of his strength and authority, had neither guarded nor prepared. His great head jerked back as though it would fly from his shoulders. And Parr, wrenching loose, followed up the advantage because a second's hesitation would be his downfall.

He hit Ling on the lower end of the breastbone, where his belly would be softest. Above him he heard the beast-giant grunt in pain, and then Parr swung roundabout to score on the jaw again. Ling actually gave back, dropping his immense bludgeon. A body less firmly pedestalled upon powerful legs and scoop-shovel feet would have gone down. It took a moment for him to recover.

"Aaaah!" he roared. "I kill you!"

Parr had stooped and caught up his own discarded club. Now he threw it full at the distorted face of his enemy. Ling's hands flashed up like a shortstop's, snatched the stick in midair, and broke it in two like a carrot. Another roar, and Ling charged, head down and arms outflung for a pulverizing grapple.

Parr sprang sidewise. Ling blundered past. His stooping head crashed against a tree, his whole body bounded back from the impact, and down he went in a quivering, moaning heap. He did not get up.

Parr backed away, gazing at the others. They stood silent in a score of attitudes, like children playing at moving statues. Then:

"Huh!" cried one. "New boss!"

A chorus of cries and howls greeted this. They gathered around Parr with fawning faces. "You boss! You fight Ling—beat 'im. Huh, you boss!"

At the racket, Ling recovered a little, and managed to squirm into a sitting posture. "Yes," he said, "you boss."

With one hand holding his half-smashed skull, he lifted the other in salute to Parr.

It took time—several days—but Parr got over his first revulsion at the bestial traits of his new companions. After all, in shedding the wit and grace of man, they were recovering the honest simplicity of animals. For instance, Ling was not malicious about being displaced, as Shanklin had been. Too, there was much more real mutual helpfulness, if not so much talk about it. When one of the horde found a new crop of berries or roots or nuts, he set up a yell for his friends to come and share. A couple of oldsters, doddering and incompetent gargoyles, were fed and cared for by the younger beast-men. And all stood ready to obey Parr's slightest word or gesture.

Thus, though it was a new thought to them, several went exploring with him to the north pole of their world. The journey was no more than fifteen miles, but took them across grassy, foodless plains which had never been worth negotiation. Parr chose Ling and another comparatively intelligent specimen who called himself Ruba. Izak, the mild-mannered one who had first met and guided Parr on the night of his banishment from the human village, also pleaded to go. Several others would have joined the party, but the deterioration of legs and feet made them poor walkers. The four went single file—Parr, then big Ling, then Ruba, then Izak. Each carried, on a vine sling, a leaf-package of fruit and a melon for quenching thirst. They also carried clubs.

The plain was well-grassed, as high as Ling's knuckled knee. Occasionally small creatures hopped or scuttled away. The beast-men threw stones until Parr told them to stop—he could not help but wonder if those scurriers had once been men. The hot sun made him sweat under his plate-armor, but not for all the Solar System would he have laid it aside.

They paused for noonday lunch in a grove of ferny trees beyond the plain, then scaled some rough lava-like rocks. In the early afternoon they came to what must be the asteroid's northern pole.

Like most of the asteroids, this was originally jagged and irregular. Martian engineers in fitting it artificially to support life, had roughed it into a sphere and pulverized quantities of the rock into soil. Here, at the apex, was a ring of rough naked hills enclosing a pit into which the sun could not look. Ling, catching up with Parr on the brow of the circular range, pointed with his great club.

"Look like mouth of world," he hazarded. "Dark. Maybe world hungry—eat us."

"Maybe," agreed Parr. The pit, about a hundred yards across and full of shadow, looked forbidding enough to be a savage maw. Izak also came alongside.

"Mouth?" he repeated after Ling. "Mmm! Look down. Men in there."

There was a movement, sure enough, and a flare of something—a torch of punky wood. Izak was right. Men were inside this polar depression.

"Come on," said Parr at once, and began to scramble down the steep, gloomy inner slope. Ling grimaced, but followed lest his companions think him afraid. Ruba and Izak, who feared to be left behind, stayed close to his heels.

The light of the torch flared more brightly. Parr could make out figures in its glow—two of them. The torch itself was wedged in a crack of the rock, and beneath its flame the couple seemed to tug and wrench at something that gleamed darkly, like a great metal toadstool at the bottom of the depression. So engrossed were the workers that they did not notice Parr and his companions, and Parr, drawing near, had time to recognize both.

One was Sadau, who would have remained his friend. The other was Varina Pemberton. In the torchlight she looked browner and more vigorous than when he had seen her last.

"What are you doing?" he called to them.

Abruptly they both snapped erect and looked toward him. Sadau seized the torch and whirled it on high, shedding light. Varina Pemberton peered at the newcomers.

"Oh," she said, "it's you. Parr. Well, get out of here."

Parr stood his ground, studying the toadstool-thing they had been laboring over. It was a wheel-like disk of metal, set upon an axle that sprouted from the floor of rock. By turning it, they could finish opening a great rock-faced panel near by....

"Get out," repeated the girl, with a hard edge on her voice.

Parr felt himself grow angry. "Take it easy," he said. "Your crowd booted me out, and I'm not under your rule any more. Neither can this be said to be your country. We've as much right here as you."

"Four of us," added Ruba with threatening logic. "Two of you. Fight, uh?"

"Parr," said Sadau, "do as Miss Pemberton tells you. Leave here."

"And if I don't?" temporized Parr, who felt the eagerness of his beast-men for some sort of a skirmish.

Varina Pemberton took something from her belt and pointed it. A brittle report resounded—whick! And an electro-automatic pellet exploded almost between Parr's feet, digging a hole in the rock. He jumped back. So did his three comrades, from whose memories had not faded the knowledge of firearms.

"The next shot," she warned, "will be a little higher and more carefully placed. Get out, and don't come back."

"They win," said Parr. "Come on, boys."

They retired to the upper combing of rock, with the sun at their backs. There Parr motioned them into hiding behind jagged boulders. Time passed, several hours of it. Finally they saw Sadau and Varina Pemberton depart on the other side of the hole.

"Good," rumbled Ling. "We follow. Sneak up. Grab. Kill."

"Not us," Parr ruled. "No war against women, Ling. But we'll go down where they were working, and see what it's all about."

They groped their way down again. At the bottom of the pit-valley they found the metal projection, so like a mighty steering wheel. Sadau's torch lay there, extinguished, and Parr still carried a radium lighter in the pocket of his shabby shorts. He made a light, and looked.

The big panel or rock, that had been half-open, was closed. As for the wheel, it had been bent and jammed, by powerful blows with a rock. He could not budge it, nor could the mighty Ling, nor could all of them together.

"They were inside this asteroid," decided Parr, half to himself. "Down where the Martians planted the artificial gravity-machinery. Having been there, they fixed things so nobody will follow them. Only blasting rays could open up a way, and those would probably wreck the mechanism and send air, water and exiles all flying into space. All this she did. Why?"

"Why what?" asked Izak, not comprehending.

"Yes, why what?" repeated Parr. "I can only guess, Izak, and none of my guesses have been worth much lately. Let's go home, and keep an eye peeled on our neighbors."

The Martians had come again—the same space-patroller, repaired, and twice as many hands and a new skipper. They carried no Terrestrial exile—for once their errand was different.

Four of them, harnessed into erect human posture, armed and armored, stood around the evening fire in the central clearing of the village now ruled by Varina Pemberton. The skipper was being insistent, but not particularly deadly.

"We rrecognize that fourr dead among you will ssettle forr one dead Marrtian," he told the gathered exiles. "The morre sso ass you assurre me that the man rresponssible hass been drriven frrom among you. But we make one demand—the arrmorr taken frrom the body of the dead Marrtian."

"I am sorry about that," the chieftainess replied from her side. "We didn't know that you valued it. If we get it back for you—"

"Ssuch action would rreflect favorrably upon you," nodded the Martian skipper. "Get the arrmorr again, and we will rrefrrain frrom punitive meassurress."

"Why do you want that armor so much?" inquired Shanklin boldly. He himself had never thought of it as worth much. He was more satisfied to have the knife, which he now hid behind him lest the Martians see and claim. But the skipper only shook his petalled skull.

"It iss no prroblem of yourrss," he snubbed Shanklin. And, to Varina Pemberton: "What time sshall we grrant you? A day? Two dayss?... Come before the end of that time and rreporrt to me at the patrol vessel."

He turned and led his followers back toward the plain where the ship was parked.

Night had well fallen, and silence hung about the vessel. Only a rectangle of soft light showed the open hatchway. The Martian officer led the way thither, ducked his head, entered—

Powerful hairy hands caught and overpowered him. Before he could collect himself for resistance, other hands had disarmed him and were dragging him away. His three companions, narrowly escaping the same fate, fell back and drew their guns and ray throwers. A voice warned them sharply:

"Don't fire, any of you. We've got your friends in here, and we've taken their electro-automatics. Give us the slightest reason, and we'll wipe them out first—you second."

"Who arre you?" shrilled one of the Martians, lowering his weapon.

"My name's Fitzhugh Parr," came back the grim reply. "You framed me into this exile—it's going to prove the worst day's work you Martian flower-faces ever did. Not a move, any of you! The ship's mine, and I'm going to take off at dawn."

The three discomfited hands tramped away again. Inside the control room, Parr spoke to his shaggy followers, who grinned and twinkled like so many gnomes doing mischief.

"They won't dare rush us," he said, "but two of you—Ling and Izak—stay at the door with those guns. Dead sure you can still use 'em?... You, Ruba, come here to the controls. You say you once flew space-craft."

Ruba's broad, coarse hand ruffled the bushy hair that grew on his almost browless head. "Once," he agreed dolefully. "Now I—many thing I don't remember." His face, flat-nosed and blubber-lipped, grew bleak and plaintive as he gazed upon instruments he once had mastered.

"You'll remember," Parr assured him vehemently. "I never flew anything but a short-shot pleasure cruiser, but I'm beginning to dope things out. We'll help each other, Ruba. Don't you want to get away from here, go home?"

"Home!" breathed Ruba, and the ears of the others—pointed, some of those ears, and all of them hairy—pricked up visibly at that word.

"Well, there you are," Parr said encouragingly. "Sweat your brains, lad. We've got until dawn. Then away we go."

"You will never manage," slurred the skipper from the corner where the Martian captives, bound securely, sprawled under custody of a beast-man with a lever bar for a club. "Thesse animalss have not mental powerr—"

"Shut up, or I'll let that guard tap you," Parr warned him. "They had mental power enough to fool you all over the shop. Come on, Ruba. Isn't this the rocket gauge? Please remember how it operates!"

The capture of the ship had been easy, so easy. The guard had been well kept only until the skipper and his party had gone out of sight toward the human village. Nobody ever expected trouble from beast-men, and the watch on board had not dreamed of a rush until they were down and secure. But this—the rationalization of intricate space-machinery—was by contrast a doleful obstacle. "Please remember," Parr pleaded with Ruba again.

And so for hours. And at last, prodded and cajoled and bullied, the degenerated intelligence of Ruba had partially responded. His clumsy paws, once so skilful, coaxed the mechanism into life. The blasts emitted preliminary belches. The whole fabric of the ship quivered, like a sleeper slowly wakening.

"Can you get her nose up, Ruba?" Parr found himself able to inquire at last.

"Huh, boss," spoke Ling from his watch at the door. "Come. I see white thing."

Parr hurried across to look.

The white thing was a tattered shirt, held aloft on a stick. From the direction of the village came several figures, Martian and Terrestrial. Parr recognized the bearer of the flag of truce—it was Varina Pemberton. With her walked the three Martian hands whom he had warned off, their tentacles lifted to ask for parley, their weapons sheathed at their belts. Sadau was there, and Shanklin.

"Ready, guns," Parr warned Ling and Izak. "Stand clear of us, out there!" he yelled. "We're going to take off."

"Fitzhugh Parr," called back Varina Pemberton, "you must not."

"Oh, must I not?" he taunted her. "Who's so free with her orders? I've got a gun myself this time. Better keep your distance."

The others stopped at the warning, but the girl came forward. "You wouldn't shoot a woman," she announced confidently. "Listen to me."

Parr looked back to where Ruba was fumbling the ship into more definite action. "Go on and talk," he bade her. "I give you one minute."

"You've got to give up this foolish idea," she said earnestly. "It can't succeed—even if you take off."

"No if about it. We're doing wonders. Make your goodbyes short. I wish you joy of this asteroid, ma'am."

"Suppose you do get away," she conceded. "Suppose, though it's a small, crowded ship, you reach Earth and land safely. What then?"

"I'll blow the lid off this dirty Martian Joke," he told her. "Exhibit these poor devils, to show what the Martians do to Terrestrials they convict. And then—"

"Yes, and then!" she cut in passionately. "Don't you see, Parr? Relations between Mars and Earth are at breaking point now. They have been for long.

The Martians are technically within their rights when they dump us here, but you'll be a pirate, a thief, a fugitive from justice. You can cause a break, perhaps war. And for what?"

"For getting away, for giving freedom to my only friends on this asteroid," said Parr.

"Freedom?" she repeated. "You think they can be free on Earth? Can they face their wives or mothers as they are now—no longer men?"

"Boss," said Ling suddenly and brokenly, "she tell true. No. I won't go home."

It was like cold water, that sudden rush of ghastly truth upon Parr. The girl was right. His victory would be the saddest of defeats. He looked around him at the beast-men who had placed themselves under his control—what would happen to them on Earth? Prison? Asylum? Zoo?...

"Varina Pemberton," he called, "I think you win."

The hairy ones crowded around him, sensing a change in plan. He spoke quickly:

"It's all off, boys. Get out, one at a time, and rush away for cover. Nobody will hurt you—and we'll be no worse off than we were." He raised his voice again: "If I clear out, will we be left alone?"

"You must give back that armor," she told him. "The Martians insist."

"It's a deal." He stripped the stuff from him and threw it across the floor to lie beside the bound prisoners. "I'm trusting you, Varina Pemberton!" he shouted. "We're getting out."

They departed at his orders, all of them. Ling and Izak went last, dropping the stolen guns they had held so unhandily. Parr waited for all of them to be gone, then he himself left the ship.

At once bullets began to whicker around him. He dodged behind the ship, then ran crookedly for cover. By great good luck, he was not hit. His beast-men hurried to him among the bushes.

"Huh, boss?" they asked anxiously. "Ship no good? What we do?"

He looked over his shoulder. Somewhere in the night enemies hunted for him. The beast-folk were beneath contempt, would be left alone. Only he had shown himself too dangerous to be allowed life.

"Goodbye, boys," he said, with real regret. "I'm not much of a boss if I bring bullets among you. Get back home, and let me haul out by myself. I mean it," he said sternly, as they hesitated. "On your way, and don't get close to me again—death's catching!"

They tramped away into the gloom, with querulous backward looks. Parr took a lonely trail in an opposite direction. After a moment he paused, tingling with suspense. Heavy feet were following him.

"Who's coming?" he challenged, and ducked to avoid a possible shot. None came. The heavy tread came nearer.

"Boss!" It was Ling.

"I told you to go away," reminded Parr gruffly.

"I not go," Ling retorted. "You no make me."

"Ling, you were boss before I came. Now that I'm gone from you—"

"You not gone from me. You my boss. Those others, they maybe pick new boss."

"Ling, you fool!" Parr put out a hand in the night, and grabbed a mighty shaggy arm. "I'll be hunted—maybe killed—"

"Huh!" grunted Ling. "They hunt us, maybe they get killed." He turned and spat over his shoulder, in contempt for all marauding Martians and their vassal Earth folk. "You, me—we stay together, boss."

"Come on, then," said Parr. "Ling, you're all right."

"Good talk!" said Ling.

They went to the other side of the little spinning world, and there nobody bothered them. Time and space were relative, as once Einstein remarked to illustrate a rather different situation; anyway, the village under Varina Pemberton numbered only eight men—Parr and Ling could avoid that many easily on a world with nearly nine hundred square miles of brush, rock and gully.

In a grove among grape-vines they built a shelter, and there dwelt for many weeks. Ling wore well as a sole friend and partner. Looking at the big, devoted fellow, Parr did not feel so revolted as at their first glimpse of each other. Ling had seemed so hairy, so misshapen, like a troll out of Gothic legends. But now ... he was only big and burly, and not so hairy as Parr had once supposed. As for his face, all tusk and jaw and no brow, where had Parr gotten such an idea of it? Homely it was, brutal it wasn't....

"I get it," mused Parr. "I'm beginning to degenerate. I'm falling into the beast-man class, closer to Ling's type. Like can't disgust like. Oh, well, why bother about what I can't help?"

He felt resigned to his fate. But then he thought of another—Varina Pemberton, the girl who might have been a pleasant companion in happier, easier circumstances. She had banished him, threatened him, wheedled him out of victory. She, too, would be slipping back to the beast. Her body would warp, her skin grow hairy, her teeth lengthen and sharpen—Ugh! That, at least, revolted him.

"Look, boss," said Ling, rising from where he lounged with a cluster of grapes in his big hand. "People coming—two of 'em."

"Get your club," commanded Parr, and caught up his own rugged length of tough torn-wood. "They're men, not beast-men—they must be looking for trouble."

"Couldn't come to a better place to find it," rejoined Ling, spitting between his palm and the half of his cudgel to tighten his grip. The two of them walked boldly into view.

"I see you, Sadau!" shouted Parr clearly, for there was no mistaking the gaunt, freckled figure in the lead. "Who's that with you?"

The other man must be a new arrival. He was youngish and merry-faced as he drew closer, with black curly hair and a pointed beard. There was a mental-motive look to him, as if he were a high grade engineer or machinist. He wore a breech-clint of woven grasses, and looked expectantly at Parr.

"They aren't armed," pointed out Ling, and it was true. The pair carried sticks, but only as staffs, not clubs.

"Parr!" Sadau was shouting back. "Thank heaven I've found you—we need you badly." He came close, and Parr hefted his club.

"No funny business," he challenged, but Sadau gestured the challenge aside.

"I'm not here to fight. I say, you're needed. Things have gone wrong, awfully. The others got to feeling that there was no reason to obey a woman chief, even though Miss Pemberton has many good impulses—"

"I agree to that," nodded Parr, remembering the girl's many strange behaviors. "I daresay she wasn't much of a leader."

Sadau did not argue the point. "Shanklin, as the previous newest man, grabbed back the chieftaincy," he plunged ahead. "Those other fools backed him. When I tried to defend Miss Pemberton, they drove me out. I stumbled among the others—that crowd you used to capture the patroller—and got a line on where you were. I came for help."

One phase had stuck in Parr's mind. "You tried to defend that girl. They were going to kill her?"

"No. Shanklin, as chief and king, figures he needs a queen. She's not bad looking. He's going to marry her, unless—"

Parr snorted, and Sadau's voice grew angry. "Curse it, man, I'm not casting you for a knight of the Table Round, or the valiant space-hero who arrives in the nick of time at the television drama! Simplify it, Parr. You're the only man who ever had the enterprise to do anything actual here. You ought to be chief still, running things justly. And it isn't justice for a girl to be married unofficially to someone she doesn't like. Miss Pemberton despises Shanklin. Now, do you get my point, or are you afraid?"

It was Ling who made answer: "My boss isn't afraid of anything. He'll straighten that mess out."

Parr glanced at the big fellow. "Thanks for making up my mind for me, Ling. Well, you two have talked me into something. Sadau, shake Ling's big paw. And," he now had time to view the stranger at close hand, "who's this with you?"

The man with the black curls looked genially surprised. "You know me, boss. I'm Frank Rupert."

Parr stared. "Never heard of you."

"You're joking. Why, I almost got that Martian patroller into space, when Miss Pemberton—"

Parr sprang at him and caught him by his shoulders. "You were Ruba—Rupert! It's only that you didn't talk plain before. What's happened to you, man?"

Sadau hastily answered: "The degeneration force is obviated. Reversed. All those who were beast-men are coming back, some of the later arrivals completely normal again. Haven't you noticed a change in this big husk?"

Parr turned and looked at Ling. So that was it! Day by day, the change had not been enough to impress him. As Ling had climbed back along his lost evolutionary trail, Parr had thought that he himself was slipping down....

"Don't stop and scratch your head over it, Parr," Sadau scolded him. "It'll take a lot of explaining, and we haven't time. You said you'd help get Miss Pemberton out of her jam. Come on."

It was like the television thrillers, after all, Parr reflected. But Sadau was right on one count—Parr didn't quite fill the role of the space-hero. He had neither the close-clipped moustache nor the gleaming top boots. But he did have the regulation deep, unfathomable eyes and the murderous impulse.

It was just after noon. Shanklin, as chief-king, had also set up for a priest. In the center of the village clearing, he stood holding a sullen and pale Varina Pemberton by one wrist, while he recited what garblings of the marriage service he remembered. His subordinates were gathered to leer and applaud. They did not know of the rush until it was all over them.

Parr smote one on the side of the neck and spilled him in a squalling heap. Sadau, Ling and Rupert overwhelmed the rest of the audience, while Parr charged on into Shanklin. His impact interrupted the words "I take this woman" just after the appropriate syllable "wo". As once before with Ling, Parr dusted Shanklin's jaw with his fist, followed with a digging jab to the solar plexus, and swung again to the jaw. Shanklin tottered, reeled back, and Parr closed in again.

"I always knew I could lick you," Parr taunted. "Come on and fight, bridegroom. I'll raise a knot on your head the size of a wedding cake."

Shanklin retreated another two paces, and from his girdle snatched the Martian knife. He opened its longest blade with a snap. Varina Pemberton screamed. Then, above the commotion of battle, sounded the flat smack of an electro-automatic. Shanklin swore murderously, dropping his knife. His knuckles were torn open by the grazing pellet.

And Parr, glancing in the direction whence the shot came, realized with savage disgust that the space-hero had come after all. There stood a gorgeous young spark in absolutely conventional space-hero costume, not forgetting the top-boots or the close-clipped moustache. Parr moved back, as if to allow this young demigod the center of the stage.

But Varina Pemberton was not playing the part of heroine. Instead of rushing in and embracing, she set her slim hands on her hips. She spoke, and her voice was acid: "It's high time you came, Captain Worrall. I did my part of the job weeks ago."

The handsome fellow in uniform chuckled. "We weren't late, at least. We've been hiding here for some time—saw what this fellow I shot loose from the knife had in mind whole hours ago. But we also saw these others," and he nodded toward Parr. "They sneaked up in such a business-like manner, I hadn't the heart to spoil their rescue."

Other uniformed men—hands of the Terrestrial Space Fleet—were coming into view from among the boughs. They, too, were armed. Ling walked across to Parr, a struggling captive under each arm.

"What are these strangers up to, boss?" he demanded. "Say the word and I'll wring that officer's neck. I never liked officers, anyway."

"Wait," Parr bade him. Then, to the man called Captain Worrall: "Just what are you doing here?"

"This asteroid," replied Worrall, "is now Terrestrial territory. We're fortifying it against the Martians. War was declared three weeks ago, and we made rocket-tracks for this little crumb. It's an ideal base for a flanking attack."

Parr scowled. "You're fortifying?" he repeated. "Well, you'd better shag out of here. There's a power—not working just now, but—"

"No fear of that," Varina Pemberton told him. She was smiling.

"I can explain best by starting at the start. Recently we got a report of what the Martians were doing out here. We realized that Earth must take care of her own, these poor devils who were being pushed back into animalism. Also, with war inevitable—"

"You aren't starting at the start," objected Parr. "Where do you fit into all this? You're no soldier."

"Oh, but she is," Captain Worrall said, offering Parr a cigarette from a platinum case. "She's a colonel of intelligence—high ranking. Wonderful job you've done, Colonel Pemberton."

She took up the tale again: "If the reverse-evolution power could be destroyed, this artificially habitable rock in space would be a great prize for our navy to capture. So I took a big chance—got myself framed to a charge of Murder on Mars, and was the first woman ever sent here. I knew fairly accurately when war would break out, and figured I had months to do my work in. That captured armor gave me the clue."

"All I knew was that it gave off a vibration," nodded Parr.

"Exactly. Which meant that the evolution-reverse was vibratory, too. I confided in Sadau, and he and I pieced the rest of the riddle together. The vibrator would be inside, where nobody would venture for fear of jamming the gravity-core—but we ventured—"

"And shut it off!" cried Parr.

"More than that. We reversed it, started it again at top speed to cause a recovery from the degeneration process. Clever, these Martians—they fix it so you can shuttle to and fro in development. Already the higher beast-men are back to normal, like Rupert there, and the others will be all right, soon."

"You had every right to chase me off at the end of a pistol," said Parr. "I might have gummed the works badly."

"You nearly did that anyway," Varina Pemberton accused. "Fighting, raiding, stirring up the Martians who might have put a crimp in my plans any moment—but, being the type you are, you couldn't do otherwise. I recognized that when I gave you the protective armor."

He gazed at her. "Why didn't you keep it for yourself?"

"No," and she shook her tawny head. "I figured to win or lose very promptly. But you, armored against degeneration, might live after me and be an awful problem to the Martians. Remember, I didn't make you give it back until I had done what I came to do."

Worrall spoke again: "Colonel, these exiles must stay until all effects of the degeneration influence is gone. They'll figure as civilians, with colonists' rights. That means they must have a governor, to cooperate with the military garrison. Will that be you?"

Shanklin dared to speak: "I am chief—"

"Arrest that man," the girl told two space-hands. "No, Captain. But I'm senior officer, and I'll make an appointment. By far the best fitted person for the governorship is Fitzhugh Parr."

The other exiles had pressed close to listen. Sadau, the diplomatic, at once set up a cheer. Ling added his own loyal bellow, and the others joined in. Parr's ears burned with embarrassment.

"Have it your way," he said to them all. "We'll live here, get normal, and help all we can. But first, what have we to eat? We've got guests."

"No, governor, you're the guest of the garrison," protested Captain Worrall. "Come aboard my ship yonder. I'll lend you a uniform, and you'll preside at the head of the table tonight."

"Varina Pemberton," Parr addressed the girl who had caused so much trouble and change on the little world of exile, "will you come and sit at my right hand there?"

"A pleasure," she smiled, and put her arm through his.

Everybody cheered again, and both Parr and the girl blushed.

www.ingramcontent.com/pod-product-compliance
Lightning Source LLC
Chambersburg PA
CBHW050913120626
46552CB00004B/1548